Shu-Li
and the
Magic Pear Tree

Shu-Li
and the
Magic Pear Tree

By
Paul Yee

Illustrated by
Shaoli Wang

Vancouver London

Published in Canada, the US and the UK in 2017

Text copyright © 2017 by Paul Yee
Illustrations copyright © 2017 by Shaoli Wang
Book & cover design by Jacqueline Wang

Inside pages printed on FSC certified paper using vegetable-based inks.

2 4 6 8 10 9 7 5 3 1
Printed in Canada

Cataloguing-in-Publication Data for this book
is available from The British Library.

Library and Archives Canada Cataloguing in Publication

Yee, Paul, author
Shu-Li and the magic pear tree / Paul Yee ; with illustrations by
Shaoli Wang.

ISBN 978-1-926890-15-9 (paperback)

I. Wang, Shaoli, 1961-, illustrator II. Title.

PS8597.E3S583 2016   jC813'.54   C2016-905396-2

For Clara,
our Family Phoenix
—PY

To Shirley,
for our friendship over the years
—SW

The publisher wishes to thank Jullia Heller for her help editing this book.

The publisher acknowledges the support of the Canada Council for the Arts.

 Canada Council **Conseil des Arts**
for the Arts **du Canada**

The publisher also wishes to thank the Government of British Columbia for the
financial support it has extended through the book publishing tax credit program
and the British Columbia Arts Council.

The publisher also acknowledges the financial support of the Government of
Canada through the Book Publishing Industry Development Program (BPIDP)
and the Association for the Export of Canadian Books (AECB) for our publishing
activities.

Chapter One

It was the end of summer. Next week, Shu-Li and Tamara would be returning to school.

"You seem sad," Shu-Li said, as the two girls walked up the Drive.

"The summer is over," Tamara replied, stopping by the window of a toy shop. "Now it's back to books and homework. What are you reading now to Mrs Rossi?"

"*Call of the Wild*." Shu-Li reached into her backpack and took out the book. Its cover featured a lean grey wolf, muzzle raised and jaws open showing two rows of sharp teeth.

"That book's for boys . . . and it looks like it's a hundred years old."

"And she's probably a hundred years old too," Shu-Li said.

Both girls giggled.

"She likes me to read her the books she read when she was growing up."

At the start of the summer, on the last day of school, Mr Ortega had asked if any students wanted to do volunteer work. He called it DEED OF THE WEEK. Shu-Li was assigned to read to Mrs Rossi, a widow who lived alone in an old house nearby. Tamara and Diego were assigned to help the activity coordinator in a seniors' tower on the Drive.

At the crosswalk, the girls waited for the traffic signal to change. A trolley bus rumbled by, its side plastered with advertisements for cell phones.

"Thanks for helping me read to Mrs Rossi today," Shu-Li said. "I'm going to keep reading to her one day a week even though school is starting. Maybe you can read to her, too."

"That would be fun."

They started walking up the hill to Victoria Drive.

"I would have kept doing my volunteer work too," Tamara said, "if they'd let me. Why doesn't Mrs Rossi move to the seniors' tower?"

"She likes living in her house. Her father built it," answered Shu-Li. "Then she and her husband raised a family there. That place means a lot to her."

"How old is she really?"

"Old enough to tell great stories."

• • •

Shu-Li banged the brass knocker on the door. Right away, the door swung open. Mrs Rossi had been waiting for them.

"Welcome, welcome," she sang out, ushering the girls in. She was a small woman, and she wore a simple black dress with broad stripes. Thick glasses framed her eyes. Her grey-white hair was loosely tied behind her neck. She wore sensible shoes and walked carefully with the help of a cane.

The girls stepped gingerly into the living room. The sofa and chairs around the dusty fireplace were covered with colourful woolen throws.

"She must love to knit," Tamara whispered to Shu-Li.

Mrs Rossi gestured for the girls to follow her through the dining room—the big table was cluttered with tin boxes, potted plants and cards from birthdays and Mother's Day—into the kitchen, bright with many windows.

Mrs Rossi took a pitcher of juice from the kitchen table and stepped through the back door onto the porch. "Shu-Li, bring three glasses out here with you, dear!"

"Wow!" breathed Tamara, stepping out onto the porch. "You have an amazing view!"

"That's why they call this area 'Grandview,'" Mrs Rossi said.

The house offered a splendid panorama of downtown Vancouver, the sports stadium and rows and rows of glass towers. The Skytrain line snaked out toward the Drive. The neighbourhood had narrow lots, so Mrs Rossi's back yard was long, and lined with flowering bushes and mature trees. On one of the trees was a tree-house perched on sturdy branches.

"Are those pears ripe?" Tamara asked, pointing at one tree.

"Yes, they're ready for picking."

"Mrs Rossi," Shu-Li said, "school is starting, and I won't be able to come twice a week anymore. So can Tamara read to you too?"

"I live close by," Tamara chimed in. "Just a few houses away."

"My wish has come true!" exclaimed Mrs Rossi. "I was just telling myself this morning, 'Oh how I wish Shu-Li would keep reading to me. I so enjoy those old books.'"

"Do you think wishes really can come true?" Tamara asked.

"Of course," Mrs Rossi grinned. Her eyes brightened. "There are many stories where wishes come true. I told them to my children

when they were young. Don't you girls believe in magic?"

"I do," Shu-Li said, pouring juice into a glass. "Can you tell us one of those stories, please?"

Mrs Rossi shaded her eyes with one hand and squinted at her back yard. "You know, that pear tree reminds me about one of my grandmother's tales."

"Will you tell it to us?" Tamara asked.

"Of course. Now I have no choice."

• • •

Long ago a poor family lived on a farm, far from town and far from the forest. The family worked hard, tending field potatoes, garden vegetables and fruit trees. They only had a few sticks of furniture but were very content.

The parents dearly loved their daughter, who helped tend the farm. She loved to water the vegetables and pick fruit.

One winter, the north wind kept blowing and the sun never showed its face. It was so cold that the family burned two and three times the amount of firewood to keep warm. Then, on the coldest day, the family ran out of fuel.

"I'll go chop down some fruit trees," said Father.

"No!" cried Daughter. "Trees are my dearest friends."

"Your mother is going to have a baby," Father said, "and she must keep warm."

"Please," Daughter begged. "Don't cut down the fruit trees. In spring, they blossom and the flowers feed the bees, which give honey. In fall, the fruit feeds us all winter long."

"Then what shall we do?"

"I know," she said. "Let's burn that chair."

They broke it apart and tossed it into the stove, and the flames danced high.

Then, Father and Daughter took down the empty shelves and burned the planks of wood.

"Now there's nothing left to burn," Mother said, shivering and pulling a blanket around her shoulders.

Daughter said, "I have something to burn."

She brought out three wooden pears. Grandfather had carved them long ago as a birthday gift. "They will bring you good luck," he had said.

"Are you sure?" Father asked.

"Those wooden pears look real enough to eat."

"I worry more about the trees," she said.

Daughter popped the wooden pears into the stove and started to weep. Soon Father would go chop down the fruit trees.

"Daughter, come!" Father called. "The pears are burning but not turning into ash." The three pears stayed round and plump, glowing like red-hot coals.

"It's magic!"

The next year's crop of pears was twice as large, twice as sweet and twice as juicy. And no winter was ever as cold, so the family always had firewood.

• • •

"Is that story true?" Tamara asked.

"It happened to my Nonna," replied Mrs Rossi. "My grandmother."

"Is your pear tree magic too?" asked Shu-Li.

"Sometimes yes, sometimes no." Then she said, "School is about to start again, so would you like to invite your friends to see my garden and its grand view?"

"They'll love the tree-house!" exclaimed the girls.

Chapter Two

"Shu-Li, your group reports first," announced Ms Abdul.

Nika James, a new student, and Tamara, Joey and Diego were talking and paid no attention to their new teacher. The class was abuzz with clusters of kids eagerly chatting. Ms Abdul had just divided them into five groups to research the province's many First Nations. They were to have meetings over the next weeks, and then each group would do a presentation to the class. Shu-Li's group had chosen to focus on the St'at'imc nation.

"It's pronounced 'Stat-liem,'" announced Nika, "and its territory is huge. It's got so many trees and mountains and the Fraser River too. My reserve is near Lillooet. And this summer, I started a new hobby, hoop dancing."

She gave a quick demonstration, stretching her arms out sideways and dipping them up and then down in a straight line while shuffling her feet. Then she sat down, smiling.

Shu-Li liked her right away. She was so outgoing.

The bell rang. Joey and Diego grabbed their backpacks and raced for the door.

"Hey, wait!" shouted Nika. "We need a meeting."

"I gotta go." Joey held out his cell phone. "I'm late. Text me."

"Yeah," said Diego, doing the same. "You guys have my number?"

When he turned to give Shu-Li his number, she muttered, "Don't have a cell."

"Then get one," Joey retorted. "Everyone has one."

"I don't have one either." Tamara poked her chin up. "A lot of kids don't. My mom says that people need time off from computers and gadgets."

Shu-Li was quiet, feeling small as a beetle. Her parents agreed with Tamara's mom. Kids didn't need cell phones.

"Let's talk tomorrow morning, first thing, okay?" said Diego.

The boys ran off before the girls could answer.

Nika shook her head, annoyed. "Those idiots."

Tamara dumped her books into her backpack. "I have to rush home."

Shu-Li and Nika frowned.

"What's wrong with her?" asked Nika. "She's never around anymore."

The past few days, after school had started, the three of them hung around together. It was fun showing Nika around the neighbourhood.

"Hey, Shu-Li, why don't you come see my hoop dance?" said Nika. "Maybe I can dance as part of our presentation."

•••

Steady drumming and loud chanting filled the gymnasium. Nika removed her shoes and joined in with the dancers, who spread out everywhere. Shu-Li sat on the floor to watch.

Holding four, five or six large hoops, the dancers stepped and swayed to the music. They began to twist the hoops around their bodies, and hold them in designs—some like flowers, others like birds' wings. Once the hoops locked into place and took full form, each dancer looked like a giant. They kept moving their hands and feet as the hoops shifted from one shape to another to tell a story.

Time raced by. Soon the coach blew his whistle and the dancers dragged their hoops over to the storage room.

"Guess what?" Nika said to Shu-Li, breathless. "A famous hoop dancer is coming to do a workshop here in Vancouver. Each school gets to pick two students to take part. I hope I get to go."

Chapter Three

After Shu-Li told the group about the tree-house, everyone agreed to meet at Mrs Rossi's to discuss their project.

Shu-Li and Tamara arrived first and then Diego and his dog. "Paco's been sick all week," said Diego. "I didn't want to leave him at home."

Tamara patted Paco lightly on his forehead, and he licked her hand.

Finally Joey and Nika arrived, so Shu-Li rapped on the door and introduced her friends to Mrs Rossi.

• • •

On the back lawn, Paco ran around in small circles. Mrs Rossi took an instant liking to him.

Then, after everyone had climbed up into the tree-house and stomped on its sturdy boards, and climbed back down, they all sat down on the lawn to start the meeting.

Nika planned to research Aboriginal canoes and show how they affected the fur trade.

Diego wanted to draw a big map of St'at'imc territory. Tamara was interested in how the gold rush affected the Native people and their lands.

Just when Joey started to speak, Paco started choking, trying to cough up something. Then he threw up a frothy mix of white and brown.

"Gross!" The kids grabbed their notebooks and moved back.

Tamara fetched a scoop and brush, bag and water from the house. Paco lay on his side, panting, two front legs together and two rear legs together.

Diego petted him and looked around to apologize. "Last week, we went to the vet and she said he had a stomach infection. She gave him pills and he was getting better . . . until now."

The kids dragged their backpacks to the shade of the fruit trees. Diego lay Paco down carefully and covered him with his jacket.

Joey started to speak but Diego interrupted, yelling, "Ouch!"

His hands flew to his head, and he rolled onto his side as if wounded.

A pear had fallen on him! He grabbed it and took a big bite.

"So sweet!" he said, as juice dribbled down his chin.

The pear wasn't large, and he finished it, seeds and all, in a few bites.

"You ate the seeds?" Joey was grinning. "Trees will grow out of your nose."

"No," said Tamara, "leaves will poke out of your belly button!"

Paco moaned as if in deep pain. Diego reached over and rubbed Paco's stomach. "Poor puppy," he said, clicking his tongue. "Hard being sick, isn't it?"

He clapped his hands three times, to get Paco to stand. No luck. Then he said, "I wish Paco was as healthy as Baxter."

Baxter belonged to Mr Simpson. When he had gone to hospital, Shu-Li and Diego took care of his dog. Bigger and older than Paco, Baxter was never sick.

"C'mon, guys," called Joey. "Let's get this meeting done."

By the time they had finished, Paco was dashing around and barking. Everyone was astounded.

Nika and Tamara had him running back and forth between them, and cuddled him at every chance. Now he had lots of energy.

"Good thing Paco is well again," Shu-Li said to Diego. "Mrs Rossi told me she wants to see him again."

"He never gets better so fast after throwing up." He frowned. "So strange!"

Later, as thanks and goodbyes were being said, Mrs Rossi asked, "Who has the next turn to read to me?"

"Me," said Tamara. "Do you need stuff from the supermarket?"

"Some milk and juice, please. They're too heavy to carry."

"No problem!"

"And, Tamara, please thank your mother for that loaf of home-made bread that you brought over last time. It was delicious, just like what my Nonna used to make!"

Chapter Four

A few days later, Ms Abdul made an announcement. "Today is Shona's last day here." She gestured for Shona to come up front. "Her family is moving to Maple Ridge, and she'll be going to a new school. Our class is a little smaller now, but let's all wish her good luck."

Last year, Shona and her pals Hannah and Jenna called themselves the Nah-Nah girls and acted like the coolest kids ever. Then, Hannah moved away in the summer and now only Jenna would be left. Shu-Li saw her wipe tears from her eyes.

"I'll miss everyone," said Shona. "I really wanted to be here next week for the Moon Festival."

Before the class could stand up and shout good luck, Kalum raised his hand. "Ms Abdul, will our school be closing?"

What? A babbling of concern filled the room.

Before Ms Abdul could muster an answer, Kalum added, "My mom saw on the news that city schools have fewer kids, so the buildings aren't full. The city can save a bunch of money by closing schools."

"Kalum, you're right." The teacher's face was suddenly tense. "But, everyone listen." She

waited for quiet before speaking slowly and clearly. "This is important. Nothing final has been decided. No one knows which schools will close."

Joey said, "We might have to go to different schools."

Oh no! Friends traded glances.

"Yes, Joey, that was in the news too," said Ms Abdul. "But it may only be a rumour."

The end-of-school bell rang and the boys and girls raced off. Nika had hoop dance, Joey went for tutoring and Tamara ran off again.

Maybe she doesn't want to read to Mrs Rossi any more, Shu-Li thought. Worrying about her friend, Shu-Li hurried to the library to fetch a new book for Mrs Rossi. This time, Mrs Rossi had asked for something called *Half Magic*.

Shu-Li flipped through the pages and smiled at the illustrations. She liked books about magic.

Diego stopped when he saw her. "Guess what!" he said. "Yesterday I took Paco to the vet. She said she had never seen a little dog recover so fast from that stomach infection. She asked me what kind of food I fed him."

How strange, she thought. *Maybe there was some kind of magic in Mrs Rossi's back yard?*

Joey had been standing to one side, waiting for Diego, intently tapping on his cellphone. Now he shoved it forward. "Look! My mom just bought the latest model. Tons of new features. I get a multi-task split screen, more UI layouts and a big bunch of new emojis."

Shu-Li had no idea what he was talking about.

"Hey, Joey," Diego said, "you should sell your old phone to Shu-Li. You can make some money and she can join the modern age."

"It would be wasted," replied his friend. "It's like putting an ant in front of a wide-screen TV."

Shu-Li groaned. Joey always gave her a hard time.

I need a cellphone, she thought. *I don't care what Ba and Ma say.*

After Shu-Li had read aloud from *Half Magic* for half an hour, Mrs Rossi said it was time to take a short break.

"Please tell Diego to bring Paco for a visit," she said. "Long ago, I had a dog too."

"Did you see Paco get sick?" Shu-Li asked.

"No, but Tamara told me about it."

"Oh, you should have seen it," said Shu-Li. He got well so fast under your pear tree that I thought the fruit was magic, like in your story."

"Oh? Magic pears? Then I have another tale for you."

• • •

One cool morning long ago, a farmer loaded his fruit and vegetables onto his wagon, hitched his horse and set out for the market. The road to town passed through a dark forest.

Suddenly, from a tall tree, a bandit leapt onto the wagon, grabbed the reins and held a dagger to the farmer's throat. "Get off," he shouted, "or I will have your blood!"

The frightened farmer jumped. The bandit shook the reins and raced away.

The farmer walked on, hoping to spot the bandit in the market and have the sheriff arrest him. He passed a beggar woman huddled by the road.

"I'm so cold," she called. "Please give me your coat."

He saw her shivering and quickly handed over his coat.

She pointed to the tree branches above. "Take three pears and you can have three wishes," she said. "Each time you make a wish, toss a pear back into the forest, so that the magic stays here."

The farmer hurried on, dreaming of things to wish for—gold, more land, jewels for his wife.

Then he recalled that his wife loved that horse dearly and would be terribly upset if he didn't bring home the horse and wagon.

"I wish my horse and wagon were back here," he said, tossing a pear into the bushes.

In a flash of light, the horse, wagon and all his produce were in front of him.

But, so was the bandit! He jumped down and ran at the farmer with his dagger.

"I wish I had that dagger," shouted the farmer, hurling a second pear.

In a flash of light, the dagger was in his hand, pointing at the bandit's throat.

"Don't move," said the farmer. With his third pear, he made a last wish, "I wish this bandit would disappear."

In a flash of light, the man vanished. That night, when the farmer's wife heard his story, she scoffed, "You were dreaming!"

But he showed her the bandit's dagger.

"Oh," cried the wife, hugging him, "magic brought you and the horse safely home! That's the most important thing."

● ● ●

Before Shu-Li left that day, she asked for some fruit from the pear tree.

"Of course, take all you want," said Mrs Rossi. "Give them to your parents. They've been so kind, sending me dishes. I never ate much Chinese food before. It's very tasty!"

Then Shu-Li asked, "How is my friend Tamara doing with her reading?"

"Very well. We make each other laugh all the time. And what sharp eyes she has."

"Do you think she likes coming here to read?"

"Yes. And she reminded me to get that broken window in my kitchen fixed. A bad storm is coming tomorrow with high winds. I'm a bit worried rain will get into the house."

"Listen to the weather reports!" Mrs Rossi called out as she waved goodbye at the front door.

Chapter Five

Mrs Rossi was right. The next day Shu-Li had to wear her stiff yellow raincoat. Ma wanted her to wear rubber boots too, but she refused. In her backpack, she carried a few pears, hoping for a chance to test their magic powers.

The hours dashed by. The class had swimming in the morning and library time in the afternoon. In the last period, Ms Abdul circled the room, visiting each group to assess their progress with the projects. Things went well until Tamara's turn came.

To everyone's surprise, she had nothing to show. No outline, no plan of action. Her notebooks were empty. She hadn't taken any notes during the meeting.

Ms Abdul crossed her arms and gave the group a stern look. "Haven't you been meeting regularly?"

After the bell, Shu-Li and Nika cornered Tamara in the coatroom before she could run off.

"You need help?" Nika demanded.

Tamara looked at her feet and shook her head.

"Want to change topics," asked Shu-Li, "to something easier?"

No again.

"We all want to do well, you know," Nika said.

"Tamara, tell us what's wrong!" Shu-LI insisted. "We can keep secrets."

Their friend kept refusing to say anything.

"Tamara, tell us what's wrong," Nika said.

Shu-Li moved closer to her friend. "Tamara, do you want us to fail?"

"It's nothing!" Tamara cried. Then she muttered, "I'm so embarrassed. This is stupid."

"Tell us!"

"Okay! Just stop bugging me." Tamara gazed at the window, avoiding their eyes. "The landlord raised our rent again, so we need to move, soon. I saw Mom looking on the Internet for a new place, and the only places we can afford are far away. I don't want to change schools." Her voice faltered. "All my friends are here and good stuff is always happening on the Drive."

By now they were sitting on the floor, under the shelves and coat hooks.

"That's awful." Nika pounded the floor with her fist. "I hate landlords."

"What can we do?" Shu-Li wailed. She wanted to tear at her hair.

"I'm fine." Tamara pulled away. "I didn't do my work, because I'll have to move soon."

At the doorway, she turned. "Don't tell Mrs Rossi. I don't want her to fret."

"Wait!" shouted Shu-Li. "I have an idea."

"What?" Tamara and Nika said, at the same time.

"Promise not to laugh or call me crazy? Well, remember how Paco got well so fast after throwing up at Mrs Rossi's? We were under the pear tree, right?" She paused and faced Tamara. "Well, didn't Mrs Rossi tell us her grandmother had magic pears?" Then she faced Nika. "Remember, Diego clapped his hands three times, and then he said, 'I wish Paco was as healthy as Baxter.' His wish came true, didn't it? Paco surprised everyone, even the vet."

The girls stared at her with widened eyes. They didn't say anything, so Shu-Li continued, "Tamara, all you have to do is eat one of Mrs

Rossi's pears, seeds and all, clap three times, and make a wish."

Tamara looked at Nika. "What should I do?"

Nika clapped a hand over her mouth and shook her head.

I better be right about the magic, Shu-Li thought. *Otherwise I'm going to look really stupid.*

Mrs Rossi proved right again that evening. Gale-force winds and rain hit the city. Ferry sailings were delayed. The Grandview area lost electricity when falling trees dragged down power lines. Candles were great fun, but they didn't warm Shu-Li, who wore a winter coat to bed. She hoped classes would be cancelled, but power was restored by morning, as the storm had passed.

As Shu-Li and Nika walked into the school, Tamara ran up to them, smiling and breathless.

"The magic pear worked. My wish came true. I don't have to move away!"

Nika's mouth fell open with astonishment. Shu-Li felt like jumping up and down.

"Tell us, tell us," they cried.

"Last night our lights went out, so we lit candles." The words tumbled out. "I wondered if Mrs Rossi had any. Then I remembered her broken window. Mom made me take over some food. Mrs Rossi was so surprised to see me. Sure enough, the window was stuck, and rain had poured in. The house had no heat, so I made a fire in the fireplace. I phoned Mom and asked to stay the night. She spoke to Mrs Rossi and then said yes, so we wrapped ourselves in shawls and talked and dozed all night. I must have mentioned moving, because Mrs Rossi phoned this morning and asked Mom and I if we would like to move into her house. The rent will be low, and we can help take care of her."

"Remember," Shu-Li whispered, "this is our secret."

"How many wishes are left?" asked Nika.

"Only one more wish," answered Shu-Li. She felt embarrassed to admit she wanted to use the final wish to get a cellphone. It seemed so selfish.

• • •

Later that day, Tamara came to Nika's hoop dance class and sat with Shu-Li. The drumming and chanting gave great energy to the kids. Everyone had improved, laughing and shouting out to each other as they danced.

For the workshop try-out, Nika had created a routine with complicated moves. It was beautiful to watch, but not easy. Hoops kept slipping out of place. The coach spent time with her, breaking down the moves.

After the whistle ended the session, she looked grim and tired. Without a word, the three girls walked along, outside.

Nika kicked a stone along the sidewalk in front of her. "I know this routine. I did it perfectly for days. The try-out's on Monday. It looks bad for me."

"You have the weekend to practise," said Tamara.

"I don't know what's wrong," Nika grumbled, kicking the stone into a wall. "I practised and practised. I should be getting better, not worse."

"At the last minute," Shu-Li said, "everything will come together."

"Eat a good breakfast," Tamara advised.

"Or," said Shu-Li, "try this."

She rummaged in her backpack, through her clothes and her leftover lunch, and handed Nika a pear.

Chapter Six

On Monday morning, Shu-Li and Tamara sat side by side, deep in thought about Nika.

After the daily messages on the loudspeaker, Kalum raised his hand and asked, "Ms Abdul, is it true that our school is on the list of schools to be closed?"

"Yes, Kalum, it's true." She swallowed hard. "Our school is on that list. But the school board is organizing a hearing so people in the neighbourhood can give their views. The board members could change their mind."

Shu-Li and Tamara fretted all morning. What if they were assigned to different schools? Would the new school have a swimming pool like theirs? Maybe the school board didn't know about the special Aboriginal program at their school. Where would Ms Abdul go to teach?

At recess, they ran straight to the playground, away from everyone.

"Are you thinking what I'm thinking?" asked Tamara.

"But we gave the last magic pear to Nika," Shu-Li said.

"What bad timing."

A helicopter rumbled overhead, its rotors pounding.

"Maybe she hasn't used her wish yet. We have to find her. Now!"

They ran to the office, trying to look like they weren't running, and stood in line for the telephone. They punched in Nika's cell number, but got her recorded message. They tried again without success.

"The Aboriginal consultant, won't she know?"

They darted up the stairs, two steps at a time, to the staff room.

"Sorry, girls," said the teacher who opened the door. "She's gone to the dentist."

They sprinted to the gym to ask the hoop dance coach or musicians. But no one there knew where Nika was.

"What a mess!" Shu-Li stamped her foot.

"Office," cried Tamara. "Bulletin board! Let's find out where the try-outs are being held."

They rushed back to the office. Visitors were standing around talking to the school secretary. There were notices for an Aboriginal Harvest Festival and First Nations Library, but nothing about the try-outs.

Diego came out from the back office. He was on student duty. "Hey, what are you guys doing here?"

"Was there a flyer for the hoop dance try-outs?" Tamara asked.

"Why do you ask?" asked Diego.

After the girls explained, he said, "I just cleared the bulletin board. Check the recycle bin."

"Found it! The try-outs are today from 10 to 5 at the Cultch."

"There's still time to save our school from being closed!"

With a glance at the office clock, Diego shouted, "Hurry!"

They raced outside and through the parking lot. They waited impatiently at the traffic light. The road led north to the Cultch, an old movie house, now converted for plays and concerts. It was four blocks, three blocks, two blocks, one block away. They burst into the lobby, gasping for breath. Empty. They yanked the door into the hall and shouted, "Nika!"

The auditorium was pitch black. Only the distant stage was softly lit. Coming in from the brightness outside, the kids couldn't see clearly. But they heard drumming and chanting.

"Nika!" they screamed.

She came running through the dark and pulled them to the lobby. She danced around them, whooping with joy. "I got in. I got a spot for the workshop!"

No! Shu-Li and Tamara sagged. Too late. The last wish was gone.

But Nika wasn't finished. "I didn't eat the pear. I practised all weekend. This morning I told myself that if I believed in myself, then I'd get in. And that's just what happened."

From her bag, she pulled out the pear and gave it back to Shu-Li.

Chapter Seven

After school that same day, in the corner of the playground, the four friends gathered without Joey, who had gone to tutoring.

"Ready to make the wish?" asked Shu-Li, gripping the pear.

"Are we all taking a bite?" Tamara looked around the circle of faces.

"Four voices will make the wish stronger," said Nika.

"But, those other times, just one person made a wish," said Diego, bouncing against the chain-link fence. "Are we allowed to change the rules?"

They all fell silent.

"Besides," said Diego, "this time the wish is way bigger."

A long pause followed. Shu-Li tucked the pear into her backpack. Her mouth tightened.

Tamara and Diego glanced at each other but didn't say anything.

The next morning, Shu-Li walked to school extra early so that no one would see the big flat box she carried with her. She waited outside the classroom until Ms Abdul arrived. Of course Ms Abdul was surprised, but after hearing Shu-Li's idea, she helped to hide the box. Later, Shu-Li whispered to Jenna and Kalum.

After recess, those two went to the front of the class and explained about the planet moving around the sun, changing seasons, autumn festivals and harvest moons. Cultures around the world gave thanks in different ways for the harvest. Kalum and Jenna showed big diagrams and colourful pictures, and the two did a small parade with Chinese lanterns. Then Jenna said, "A special treat for the Chinese holiday is the moon cake. Now we have something special for everyone."

Ms Abdul brought out the big flat box. Everyone crowded around the table.

"My dad baked a moon cake," Shu-Li said. "It's really a pie made from pears. He drew a moon cake design on it."

The pie crust was golden brown, and her dad had used long thin lines of red icing to sketch two fish with big eyes, bumpy scales and fan tails. They formed a circle, with each fish head at the other's tail. The intricate border was rows and rows of tiny petals.

"I didn't know your dad was an artist too," said Tamara.

Everyone had a slice. Before they returned to their seats, Shu-Li said, "During the Harvest Moon, some people in China make a wish for something special. Want to try?"

A few of the kids said, "Sure!"

"Yesterday we heard that our school might be closed," she continued. "Let's wish for our school to be saved, okay?"

Nika and Tamara shouted, "We wish that our school is saved!" Then the girls clapped three times and the entire class joined in a chorus, "We wish that our school is saved!"

That afternoon, Joey raised his hand and said, "Ms Abdul, do you think our wish will come true?"

"I hope so. No one can predict the future, Joey."

"I just want to be sure," he said sullenly.

"Then maybe you should do more," Nika called from her side of the room.

"Do what?" demanded Joey, turning to face her. "We're just kids."

"Don't you know?" Nika said. "If you really want something, you have to work hard at it."

"I do work hard," he insisted. "Just tell me what to do."

"Ms Abdul," Nika called, "you said the school board was coming here to listen to people. Can kids go talk to them too?"

"Of course."

"Let's do it," Shu-Li cried. "Let's figure out what to say."

Chapter Eight

Several weeks galloped by before the evening of the school board meeting at the Cultch.

A huge crowd gathered at the school, including students from several grades, their parents, teachers and many supporters. All the Britannia Library staff showed up too. Everyone was excited.

A group of Aboriginal drummers and singers, adults and youngsters led the way outside. Some of them wore traditional Native clothes. The drumming and chanting filled the air.

At the Drive, the parade turned north. People on the street followed them, and drivers in cars honked their horns.

Behind the musicians came Nika and her friends, hoisting a large cardboard model of an Aboriginal canoe. Long and narrow, it needed four people to carry it. The prow swept up like the blade of a knife. Nika and Diego had built it for their class project, copying museum pictures on the Internet. They painted it black and then added a raven design in red, white and black on two sides of the front. Passersby pushed their way in, pointing their cellphones to take photos and videos.

Next came long lines of students. On their shoulders they carried paddles made from wooden poles and cardboard. On one side of the paddle was their slogan SOS–Save Our School. On the other side was some Aboriginal artwork.

The traffic light turned red against them, but the parade kept going, forcing cars to wait.

Parents and residents followed with home-made placards that read, Kids Come First and This Community Cares.

At the Cultch, CBC TV news cameras were recording everything. On the stage, the school

board members sat behind tables. Microphones were everywhere. The hall was brightly lit and packed. The drummers and singers marched down the aisle, followed by the news cameras. At the front, the musicians turned around and looked back at the door.

"Now!" shouted Diego.

Kalum and Jenna put down a big roll of paper. Then they started unrolling it, running down the aisle alongside the scroll. Kalum grabbed a microphone and said, "This is our petition to save our school. It has more than 3000 signatures."

The audience applauded. Joey came out and ran down to the front, bending over to re-roll the scroll into a neat bundle.

The drummers and singers started their music again. The students marched in with their canoe and paddles. Joey placed the petition roll into the boat, and the students carried it onto the stage. They put the canoe right in front of the school board members and said, "Now, will you listen?"

And they did.

A few weeks later, Ms Abdul brought good news to the class. "The school board has revised its list of schools to be closed. Our school will stay open."

Everyone cheered. The boys thumped their fists on the tables.

Shu-Li nudged Nika and Tamara and whispered, "What do you think? Was it the magic pear or was it the extra work?"